Bolivia

France

Replacement costs will be
billed after 42 days overdue.

India

China

The art was created with a box of
120 Crayola crayons,
22 Crayola Twistables, and
a box of 30 Swiss Neocolor I crayons
by Caran d'ache
on top of copies of pencil drawings.

DIAL BOOKS FOR YOUNG READERS
A division of Penguin Young Readers Group
Published by The Penguin Group
Penguin Group (USA) Inc., 375 Hudson Street, New York, NY 10014, U.S.A.
Penguin Group (Canada), 90 Eglinton Avenue East, Suite 700, Toronto, Ontario, Canada M4P 2Y3
(a division of Pearson Penguin Canada Inc.)
Penguin Books Ltd, 80 Strand, London WC2R 0RL, England
Penguin Ireland, 25 St. Stephen's Green, Dublin 2, Ireland (a division of Penguin Books Ltd)
Penguin Group (Australia), 250 Camberwell Road, Camberwell, Victoria 3124, Australia
(a division of Pearson Australia Group Pty Ltd)
Penguin Books India Pvt Ltd, 11 Community Centre, Panchsheel Park, New Delhi - 110 017, India
Penguin Group (NZ), Cnr Airborne and Rosedale Roads, Albany, Auckland 1310, New Zealand
(a division of Pearson New Zealand Ltd)
Penguin Books (South Africa) (Pty) Ltd, 24 Sturdee Avenue, Rosebank,
Johannesburg 2196, South Africa
Penguin Books Ltd, Registered Offices: 80 Strand, London WC2R 0RL, England

Text copyright © 2007 by Alice B. McGinty
Illustrations copyright © 2007 by Wendy Anderson Halperin
All rights reserved
The publisher does not have any control over and does not
assume any responsibility for author or third-party websites or their content.

Designed by Jasmin Rubero
Text set in Calligraphic 421
Printed in Hong Kong on acid-free paper

3 5 7 9 10 8 6 4 2

Library of Congress Cataloging-in-Publication Data
McGinty, Alice B.
Thank you, world / Alice B. McGinty ; illustrated by Wendy Anderson Halperin.
p.   cm.
Summary: A child is thankful for the special things in life, such as sun that colors the sky,
clouds that paint cotton pictures, and stars that shine like Mommy's eyes.
ISBN 978-0-8037-2705-2
[1. Nature—Fiction. 2. Stories in rhyme.] I. Halperin, Wendy Anderson, ill. II. Title.
PZ8.3.M47847453Tha 2007   [E]—dc22   2005028225

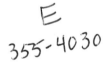
To Rosalind Poor, in fond memory
—A.B.M.

To every time "thank you" is said or thought here in the U.S. and all over the world:
in China "doh je," in Mali "minkari," in India "vandane," in Mexico and Bolivia
"muchas gracias," in France "merci," and in Saudi Arabia "shukran."
And to the barn swallow who lives (almost) worldwide.
—W.A.H.

THANK YOU, WORLD

Alice B. McGinty

illustrated by Wendy Anderson Halperin

Dial Books **for Young Readers**

Thank you, sun, for waking up the morning

and coloring the sky.

Thank you, sky, for shining blue that calls me

to touch you, swinging high.

Thank you, swing. You shoot me like a rocket

past birds and grass and trees.

Thank you, grass, for softening my footsteps.

I'm dancing with the breeze.

Thank you, breeze, for lifting up my kite wings

past treetops tall and proud.

Thank you, trees. Your branches are my playhouse.

I'm climbing to the clouds!

Thank you, clouds, for painting cotton pictures

and sending cool, sweet rain.

Thank you, rain, for watering my flowers

and washing my windowpane.

Thank you, window. You welcome in the moonlight

that yawns from starry skies.

Thank you, stars, for sparkling so brightly.

You shine like Mommy's eyes.

Thank you, Mommy, for tucking in my tiptoes

and kissing me good night.

And thank you, nighttime. Your soft gray shadows

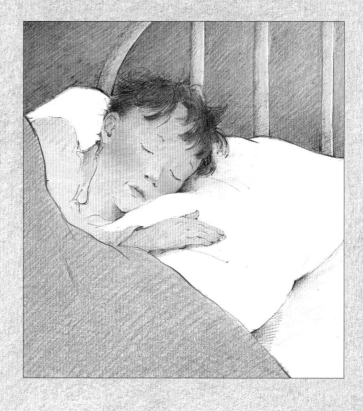

will touch my dreams tonight.

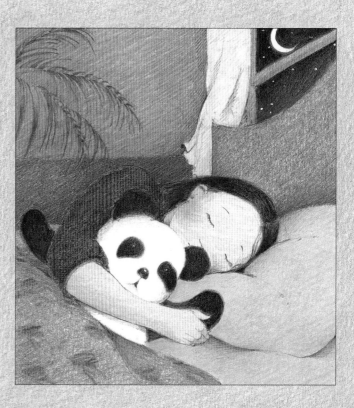

United States

Mexico

Mali

Saudi Arabia